T0321215

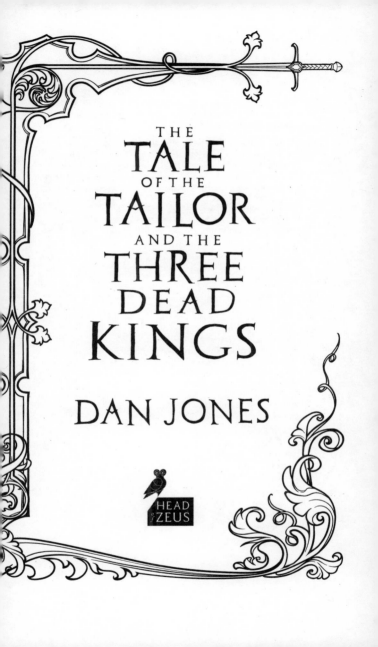

THE
TALE
OF THE
TAILOR
AND THE
THREE
DEAD
KINGS

DAN JONES

HEAD
of ZEUS

First published in the UK in 2021 by Head of Zeus Ltd

9 7 5 3 1 2 4 6 8

A catalogue record for this book is available from the British Library.

ISBN (HB): 9781801101295
ISBN (E): 9781801101301

Typeset by Francesca Mangiaracina
Illustrations by David Wardle
Frames and drop caps courtesy of Shutterstock
Image on page 84 courtesy of the British Library: Text page of ghost story from Byland, Yorkshire, England, N. (Yorkshire?), Royal 15 A XX f. 141

Printed and bound in Great Britain by
CPI Group (UK) Ltd, Croydon CR0 4YY

Head of Zeus Ltd
First Floor East
5–8 Hardwick Street
London EC1R 4RG

www.headofzeus.com

FOR DOREEN
who loves telling stories

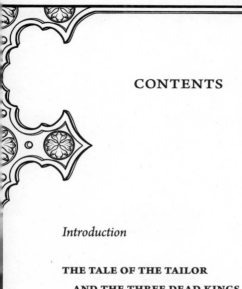

CONTENTS

INTRODUCTION

In the early 1920s the great Eton and Cambridge scholar M. R. James was leafing through a new catalogue of manuscripts in the British Museum when an unusual entry caught his eye. It concerned a five-hundred-year-old volume in the museum's 'Royal' collection. This was the name given to a set of about two thousand manuscripts, acquired slowly over the centuries by generations of English kings and queens. The texts in this collection covered all manner of topics, ranging from classical philosophy and French romance to doggerel poetry and herbal medicine. But a reference to one particular book made James sit up, for, according to the catalogue, it contained a dozen medieval ghost stories.

James had heard about these stories before. A much older list of royal manuscripts, compiled in the eighteenth century, had made fleeting mention of a volume containing 'examples of ghostly apparitions'.[1] But the new catalogue spelled out what that meant. Somewhere in the museum, under the shelf-mark 'Royal 15 A. XX', lay twelve tales of the supernatural, written down in (or shortly after) the year AD 1400 by a monk at Byland Abbey in Yorkshire. They sounded very peculiar. One concerned the ghost of a labourer who appeared 'in the shape of a horse and afterwards of a haycock' and who helped 'to carry beans'. Another told of a dead churchman from Kirkby who rose from his grave 'and blew out the eye of his concubine'. A third related how a spectre had followed a man for twenty-four miles before tossing him over a hedge.[2] The longest of the stories was about a tailor with the surname

Snowball, and his encounters with a variety of tormented spirits, who haunted him in the shapes of a raven, a dog, a goat, a bull and a huntsman and 'lastly like a dead king in the pictures'.

For James this was all too tantalizing to ignore. He hurried to get his hands on the manuscript, and when he finally inspected it, he was delighted. The stories were every bit as weird and wonderful as the catalogue promised. Sensing a scoop, James copied out all twelve and began to think of introducing them to a wider scholarly audience, via the pages of the *English Historical Review*. 'I took an early opportunity of transcribing them,' he wrote there, 'and I did not find them disappointing. I hope others will agree that they deserve to be published.'[3]

*

Today M. R. James is remembered as one of the most famous ghost-story writers in the English language. When he came across the Byland Abbey manuscript he had already published three collections of his own spooky tales. These, and others he wrote during the final years of his life, remain in print today. They have been adapted for the screen and radio numerous times since the 1950s. During my own childhood, it was traditional at Christmas for my father to screen an M. R. James film, an event that was sometimes the precursor to him playing a ghostly prank on one of the more skittish members of our family. James's stories are typically strange and fragmentary – and often end imperfectly resolved. They are popular because they are genuinely terrifying, and they are terrifying because they evoke the ragged quality of real-life experiences of the inexplicable: they give us a horrible glimpse of a hidden netherworld, but seldom the full view. The feeling they produce stays with us, even if we can never quite work out what it is we have seen.

Few people today realize that for M. R. James ghost-story writing was only a sideline. He was a serious academic, who served at various points in his life as provost of Eton College, vice-chancellor of Cambridge University and director of Cambridge's Fitzwilliam Museum. He edited scholarly editions of medieval chronicles which are still in use today (such as *De Nugis Curialium*, a colourful account of Henry II's court by the waspish Welsh diplomat Walter Map). So the Byland Abbey ghost stories combined two of his great interests. They were an intriguing oddity which James had snuffled out from England's medieval archives. But they were also unsettling accounts of the paranormal which, once read, were hard to forget. What was more, they appeared to be true. The stories, he wrote in the *English Historical Review* in 1922, 'are strong in local colour, and, though occasionally confused, incoherent and unduly compressed, evidently represent the words of the narrators with some approach to fidelity'. [4]

*

Royal 15 A. XX, which today is kept in the British Library, is a smallish bundle of 160 leaves of parchment, roughly 17 cm by 12 cm, held together in a modern binding. It is not, for the most part, a book of ghost stories at all. Rather, it is an elegantly copied compendium of texts by authors including the first-century-BC Roman orator Cicero, and several Christian theologians, including the popular high medieval writer Honorius of Autun. Most of the text was copied out in the twelfth century. But the Cistercian monks who did the copying left some blank pages. And it was on those empty leaves, in a much later generation, that the fifteenth-century ghost stories were written. The monk who penned them – we do not know his name – was a scrawler. He scratched out his letters in a cramped and crabby hand, using tortuously contracted and rather idiosyncratic late-medieval Latin. ('Very refreshing', wrote James, drily.[5])

What his purpose was in collecting twelve near-contemporary ghost stories alongside noble works by Cicero and Honorius is uncertain. It may be that the book was used in Byland Abbey as a teaching resource, from which new monks were taught about Christian doctrine; having a good ghoulish anecdote on hand amid the dustier stuff of rhetoric and theology might have been thought helpful for teachers who needed to grab their students' attention.[6] Most of the stories have an explicitly Christian flavour, with lost souls helped to pass through the afterlife after atoning for some earthly sin. So they have a didactic purpose, besides being merely entertaining. That said, it could be that the author was simply a collector of odd things, who wrote on the nearest surface to hand, like a busy modern-day parent making the weekly shopping list on the back of an electricity bill.

What is clear, though, is that the stories are closer to reportage than polished homilies: they are folk tales, circulated by the ordinary people who lived around Byland Abbey in the late fourteenth and early fifteenth centuries. They mention local landmarks and settlements: Ampleforth, Gilling, Hodge Beck, York. The author names people who experienced terrors with the undead – or sometimes, as we shall see, redacts names for fear of embarrassing their families. He assumes a certain degree of local knowledge about landscape and society.

Most of the stories are short, often just a few lines long. Without exception, they are weird. But one of them, the Snowball story, which is the second recorded and the longest by far, is a late-medieval humdinger. That is why I have adapted it for you here.

*

I came across the Byland Abbey ghost stories just before Halloween in 2020. I was looking for a scary tale from the Middle Ages with which to try and impress my children, and had a dim memory of once reading, in some northern chronicle or other, the story of a revenant. Having not much more than that to go on, I ran a few searches in online library catalogues for 'medieval ghosts'. This led me to James's article from the *English Historical Review*. It wasn't what I was looking for. (If I had thought harder, I would have remembered that it was William of Newburgh who had kept tabs on the walking dead.) But I was fascinated all the same. And, like James, one hundred years before me, I started to think that these tales deserved public airing. However, rather than retranscribing all twelve, I decided to focus on one: the story of Snowball the tailor, which I reckoned could be entertainingly adapted for twenty-first-century readers. I would not tamper with the structure or the outline, but just flesh it out here and there, developing characters a little, inventing some, even: colouring in where the Byland Abbey monk had left only sketches, and making the piece, for want of a better term, 'my own'.

In the spirit of M. R. James, who used to draft his own ghost stories longhand, to be read to small groups of friends assembled in his rooms at Eton or Cambridge, I wrote this story in one sitting. I have not tried to over-explain its eccentricities, and certainly not to analyse, but only to try and translate from the fifteenth-century original the compelling mood of horror and unease, which plays out as our protagonist, Snowball, tries to satisfy the demands of a tormented, violent and frequently rather unreasonable spirit. Where the Byland Abbey monk deliberately censored names and deeds, I have followed him; but where he simply did not mention them, I have made them up. I have invented speech and made quite a lot of an entirely fictional horse. I say again: this is a retelling. Yet at the same time I hope it conveys the marvellous spirit of the original. Readers who wish to tally the liberties I have taken can find a very good recent English translation of all the Byland stories online at www.bylandghosts.com.

For those who wish to read the stories in their original medieval Latin form, James's transcript is included at the end of this book.

James once wrote that if any of his stories 'succeed in causing their readers to feel pleasantly uncomfortable when walking along a solitary road at nightfall, or sitting over a dying fire in the small hours, my purpose in writing them will have been attained'. That would be more than good enough for me.

For now, though, it is over to Snowball the tailor.

DAN JONES
Staines-upon-Thames
Spring, 2021

1 James, M. R., 'Twelve Medieval Ghost Stories', *English Historical Review* 37 (1922), p. 413, citing Casley, David, *A Catalogue of the Manuscripts of the King's Library* (London: 1734).

2 Warner, Sir George F. and Gilson, Julius P., *Catalogue of Western Manuscripts in the Old Royal and King's Collection II* (London: 1921), pp. 147–8.

3 James, 'Twelve Medieval Ghost Stories', p. 413.

4 *Ibid.*

5 *Ibid.*

6 Hildebrandt, Maik, 'Medieval Ghosts: The Stories of the Monk of Byland' in Fleischhack, Maria and Schenkel, Elmar (eds), *Ghosts – or the (Nearly) Invisible: Spectral Phenomena in Literature and the Media* (Frankfurt: 2016), pp. 20–21.

THE
TALE
OF THE
TAILOR
AND THE
THREE
DEAD
KINGS

1

NE YEAR, a few winters back, in those dark days before King Richard[*] was put from the throne and starved in his cell till he died, Snowball the tailor was riding home on the road from Gilling to Ampleforth. It was evening: the sun was buried beneath the horizon, and the last of its light was chasing after it. The hedgerows on either side of the road were losing

[*] *King Richard II, d. 1400.*

their colour as the sky faded from brown to grey. It was November. Dank and wet and gloomy. A few leaves still hung limp on the trees, curling and rotting in place. The rest were already mulch underfoot.

Borin plodded along the murky road, picking up his hooves deliberately as though he did not like to touch the ground too long. Snowball flexed his fingers together inside his mittens, and adjusted his grip on the reins. He hated this time of year.

Over the wet clop of Borin's hooves, Snowball heard a noise. It was a sharp, croaking call – like a misfiring bagpipe wheezing from its torn bladder. Or maybe like ducks calling one another in the beck. In the spring this was a noise Snowball liked to hear. But tonight it was odd. The ducks had left the beck weeks ago. After harvest they went somewhere else. When Snowball was a boy someone had told him where it was. But he couldn't remember any more. They went, and they came back. That was all there was to it.

The path fell silent again, and Snowball sat back into his saddle and started to think of other things. His eyes and fingers ached from the day's work repairing Jack the Reeve's winter cloak, which had been eaten by worms because Jack had left it in the damp. He had a few hours more to do on it the morrow, and the cloak would have to be aired, if the weather held dry. He would—

But then the quacking started again. Louder now.

Snowball dug his heels into his horse's sides and pulled up his hood. The horse snorted and lowered its head, as though it did not like to look up. It refused to trot. Instead Borin slowed from a walk to something that was even less than that.

Snowball shivered. He looked around. The road was empty.

'Come on, Borin,' he said. ''S go.'

But Borin would not go. Snowball felt strange.

'Daft,' he said to himself, out loud. The word felt thick on his tongue.

But he knew he wasn't being daft. The quacking was now everywhere – somehow both nearer and further away, yet moving around Snowball's head from side to side. As it moved, Snowball was suddenly overtaken by the conviction that it was coming from inside him, although he knew that that was stupid talk as well.

Then from his left side the quack became

a flap and the flap became a flutter and a flurry of feathers that for a heartbeat covered everything he could see. And there was a loud thump in front of him, and suddenly the road was silent.

2

BORIN STOOD still and breathed. Snowball looked down. There, lying on the ground before him, not two yards away, was a large bird. Not a duck, but a raven. Its head and body were ink black, and its beak dull silver in the gloom. Its wings were broken, sticking out at impossible angles – one underneath its body and the other above.

It twitched a little, as though it were dying.

Snowball patted Borin's neck, and muttered in the old horse's ear. Then he swung

9

his right leg behind him and climbed down. He crouched in front of the raven and thought to himself. His father had told him ravens could mimic humans. Even mock them. But could they pretend to be ducks? Snowball wasn't sure. He stretched out his hand to touch the raven's body.

Then, from nowhere, a burst of flame erupted, which seemed to shoot from the bird to within a palm's breadth of Snowball's long nose. In shock, Snowball leapt backwards. He made the sign of the cross at his breast.

'Name of God, leave me be,' he cried out. 'Name of God, I say – Christ and the saints and the angels and all of 'em.'

The raven was starting to tremble on the ground. Snowball staggered and lunged for Borin's reins. He shot a foot out for the stirrup, and half climbed, half rolled himself up on to Borin's back, his heart hammering inside him and his bowels feeling as if they wanted to burst.

'Go, boy!' he cried to Borin, and Borin, suddenly released from his torpor, kicked up his front hooves, whinnied and reared. Ahead, the raven shot up from the road, its mangled wings propelling it skywards. As it took off, a wretched scream came from its steeled beak, a shriek like the wrenching of a felled tree. The raven flew higher and higher, and soon it had vanished into the heavens.

Borin reared again; then he set off at a gallop, Snowball clinging to his neck and whimpering, 'Name of God, name of God.' They galloped blind for what seemed like hours, although it was no more than a few moments, because just as Snowball was trying to right himself in the saddle and take back control of the panicked horse, he was hit with a tremendous blow to his right side.

Something – it felt like the heavy swing of a man-at-arms' war-hammer or a kick from a young mule – thudded into Snowball's ribs with such force that he flew clean out of his saddle and was in the air for a second before he landed heavily on his back in the road. Between the blow to the side and his hard fall to earth, Snowball had the wind knocked clean from his lungs. He lay there gasping as though he was being drowned, knowing only that he had swapped places with the raven: knowing that now he was dead, or soon to be so, and the bird, he felt certain, was looking over him, stretching out its wing as if to touch him on the cheek.

This is what it feels like to die, Snowball thought. And he did not like it much, for he did not see Jesus, or any of the saints at all, or God or anyone. So he was not sure he was ready to die. And for that reason he sat up in the road, and shook his head and blinked.

Out of the darkness the raven swooped and hit him again.

This time Snowball did not go down quite so violently, and he sat straight back up. As the raven turned to fly at him for a third time, he lashed out with his fists. He missed. But now he could feel the raven's movements, and as he sensed it loop around to hit him once more, he swung his right hand and struck the bird with every scrap of force he could muster.

It was like punching a peat-stack, and it hurt his hand very much – his stitching hand too. But Snowball felt that he had hurt the raven, so now growing confident he called out in his sternest voice: 'God forbid thee! God forbid thee!

'God forbid thou hast the power to hurt me!' he shouted. 'Begone, foul bird!'

Then he heard the horrible screaming once more, and felt a burst of air as the raven again shot skywards. After that there was silence, and Snowball sat in the road, wondering what terrible thing was going to befall him next, and if he would ever be home in Ampleforth, for he had never wanted to be there quite so badly.

He sat there for a moment like that, thinking of Ampleforth, and his little hut, and the warmth of the small fire he would make there of an evening before he curled up on his pallet. And as he did so an odd glow began to light up the road – a light that was not like anything Snowball had ever seen, for it was neither the watery reflection of the moon, nor the caress of the dawn, nor the flicker of firelight, but a sickly green light that seemed to come up from beneath the earth itself.

3

SNOWBALL LOOKED around him. Borin was nowhere to be seen. Instead, the grotesque light showed up a great dog, which padded towards Snowball on paws like hands, which spread out from blue-black legs as fat and swollen as blood puddings. The dog wore a metal collar, studded with rough nails that scratched and cut the folds of its neck. Trailing from the collar was a long iron chain, thick enough to hold a boat to its anchor. A globlet of drool hung from the beast's left jowl. Snowball smelled rotten meat. He felt sick. But for the first time since he had heard the quacking that evening, he no longer felt afraid.

'By Christ's five wounds,' said Snowball, still sitting in the road, 'tha shalt speak to me, mutt. And don't get any ideas, either. Thy friend the raven has dealt me sore enough already tonight. So tha canst answer me who th' art and what tha've done with Borin too, for I've to finish Jack the Reeve's cloak tomorrow.'

And the dog seemed to understand. It padded towards Snowball, sniffing the air around him. The acrid stench, which came from within and all around the dog, made Snowball's eyes water, but still he was not afraid. And the dog came then so close Snowball could feel its cold and clammy breath, and now he knew its scent, which was of nothing but pure and ceaseless death and of the scuttling things that live in the permanent dark.

Then the dog opened its mouth and, in a low, broken voice, it said to Snowball: 'Dost tha not recognize me, Snowball the Tailor? I am –––––, he who sinned and died excommunicate the winter last. For as tha knowst I did –––– and I did not ––––––––. And they laid my old bones in the ground unshriven, no Masses said for my soul.'

And Snowball nodded, for he remembered ––––– well. And he remembered the priest casting the candles to the church floor as the village stood together, and they all called, 'Fiat, fiat.' And he remembered when they flung –––––'s body in the hard unhallowed ground that January day, for he had charged the sexton a penny for the coarse cloth in which they wrapped the corpse, and he had heard Brom from the village laughing that it was a waste for good wool to dress a villain on his way to hell, and then seen the priest glaring and someone said, 'For shame.'

And he turned and looked to the dog, and in the green light its eyes were also green. And his hand was green and everything else too. And the dog spoke to Snowball again.

'Tha hast conjured me, Snowball,' said the dog, 'and now tha must do what I bid.

'Tha must go to York to find the priest they call Greysen and ask him to absolve me, and tha must come back then and tell me that either he will or he won't.

'Or if tha wilt not do it, then thy flesh shall rot and thy skin shall dry up and shall fall off thee utterly in a short time.'

Snowball felt something stirring inside him.

'And tha shalt not curse me,' said the dog. 'For tha knowst the reason I have met thee this night, for tha hast heard no Mass nor seen the consecration of His body today. For otherwise I would not have been able to visit thee.'

And at that Snowball felt as though his whole body were somehow on fire. The burning spread first from the tips of his fingers and his toes, and swiftly it took hold of his limbs and his private parts and his face and his back, and soon it felt that even the ends of his hair and his untidy beard were on fire. Yet when he looked at himself he was not on fire. It was the dog that was aflame – burning so fiercely that the green light now shone from within it.

And Snowball looked inside the dog's rank mouth and in it he saw the writhing mass of doggish innards, turning and twisting over one another like maggots in a bran-tub. And the dog no longer spoke with its mouth but seemed to belch forth its words from this stinking morass of guts and twining things.

'I will bring Jack the Reeve to see thee too,' he told the dog, but the dog shook its head and from its entrails it berated him.

'Tha shalt come alone, tailor,' said the dog. 'And bring with thee the four gospels, for this is a bad road for thee now, and there are two more ghosts that abide here. One burns in the hedgerow, and the other wanders the fields as a hunter.

'They are very dangerous to thee, tailor.'

And then Snowball knew quite certainly,

as sure as his name was Snowball and he could fix any garment fit for even a countess, that he was now in the dog's power.

'I'll do what tha sayst,' he said, forlornly. 'But tha must leave this road and its travellers be. Get to th' Hodge Beck and meet me there.' And he pointed across the open fields towards the Hodge Beck, where the summer ducks swam.

But at that the dog grew angry, and it threw back its head and the raven's scream burst out from its guts and its throat. So Snowball covered his ears and begged the dog to pray silence, and told it to stay, but to bother no one till he returned. And the dog continued to shriek, and the green glow grew brighter, but Snowball sensed that they now understood each other, and even as the scream grew louder, so much louder that he thought it would burst his ears, then his eyeballs, and then his skull itself, he was sure that the dog would let him go to do as he had promised.

*

And the next thing he knew he was opening his eyes on his pallet at home in Ampleforth. And the fire was stone cold, dead ashes beside his head. And Jack the Reeve was hammering at his door asking where by God's bollocks was his cloak for it was a week now Snowball had had it and the frosts were coming.

And Snowball found he was covered in sweat and very weak. He had been asleep for three days straight.

4

T WAS a long day's ride from Ampleforth to York, for the road was flooded in places, and a cold thin rain fell all the while. Borin plodded sullenly, and would not look at Snowball or respond to his pats and rubs on the neck. But they arrived before curfew and Snowball asked in the streets for the priest called Greysen, once of Ampleforth, and after he had asked a few times and been met with shrugs or just ignored outright he was pointed towards a house on the Cripplegate where Greysen now lived.

It was a falling-down place, the thatch balding and coming off in clumps, and smoke drifting out of the window for want of a good chimney that drew. Inside the house he could hear someone coughing wetly. Snowball called out and the coughing stopped and then Greysen's head poked out of the window. He looked at Snowball with pink and watery eyes; then he nodded, as though he knew what the tailor had come for before Snowball had even opened his mouth.

'Tha canst leave the nag there,' said Greysen, looking at Borin, who was eating a clump of the collapsing roof. 'They won't steal from thee here. They hang horse thieves from the walls.' And he tilted his head to the door, which was held closed with a wooden bar.

Snowball looked doubtfully at Borin, but Borin was still ignoring him. He lifted the bar and walked in.

He had barely started his story before Greysen was shaking his head, and by the time he got to asking Greysen if he might think about absolving ————— the old priest was standing up and seemed to be working up a fury.

'Tha knowst as well as I do what that godless bastard did,' said Greysen. 'Tha wast there, same as I were. Only difference is tha still art, though how tha canst stay there I don't know—'

The old priest broke off coughing. And Snowball remembered all too well. Greysen was not the only one who had left Ampleforth after that horrible time. The truth was, no one had protested when ————— had been put in the ground with God's curse still on him.

He wondered if he might leave. But then he remembered the sickly green light, and the dog with its guts and the screaming of the raven, and he looked at Greysen, who was staring at him, daring him to speak, and feeling very helpless he said: 'Can we have another opinion?'

Greysen fixed him with a glare; then he stalked out of the door into the street. He left Snowball alone, staring into the grate, where the black stumps of Greysen's wood were giving off stink and wet smoke, which in this world was what passed for a fire.

*

The vespers bells were ringing when Greysen came back. But now instead of one priest he was four, or seemed to be, for in a huddle with him were three other clerics. One was fat, one was thin and one was very ugly, with a mass of thick, stubby warts covering his face and neck, many of them red and weeping where the man had been scratching at them with his claws.

Greysen did not introduce them, but Snowball thought he recognized the thin man as Edwin, a chaplain from Gilling who had fathered several bastards on women from the village, and whose sister had died many years ago when she was bitten by a wild pig.

Greysen nodded to Edwin, and the thin man looked Snowball up and down, then said: 'A token.'

Snowball sighed. He had been expecting this. 'How much?' he said.

The thin man moved closer to him. He

peered at the window, as though he expect-
ed something to fly through it. He put a long
and gnarled finger to his lips, then flashed
both his palms twice: twenty.

Snowball shook his head. 'Sir, I …'

The thin man looked back to the others.
Greysen looked annoyed. The man with the
bloody warts cocked his head.

The thin man said it out loud. 'Twenty.'

Snowball shook his head again. 'I'm a tailor,' he said. 'I make but a shilling a week.
Two if t' work is good. Twenty shillings is
half a bloody knight's fee. You know the—'

The four clerics sighed, all together.
Greysen spoke up. 'So what hast tha got?'
he said.

Snowball held up one palm, once. Five.

Greysen rolled his rheumy eyes. 'Ten,' he
said, but in a weary voice, although he was

tired of the game already.

Snowball shook his head. 'Please, sirs,' he said. 'It's all I have.'

After Snowball had counted out his savings and been given the scrap of writing he needed, and told by all four of the churchmen not to say a word of it to anyone, nor mention ─────'s name, nor say anything of the like to anyone, the fat man and the man with the warts and the thin man maybe called Edwin all left together, and Greysen let him sleep the night in front of his chilly hearth.

In the morning he gave Snowball a meagre bowl of water and hard grain, and slopped out the same for Borin.

He told Snowball what he must do. Then he disappeared and Snowball never saw him again.

*

The paper Greysen had left Snowball was covered in symbols and strange letters, which he recognized, but could not read. And even if he had been able to read better than he could, which was not very well, he felt he still would not have understood the words. They curled round each other in patterns and shapes, intersecting in crosses and forming circles. They looked as though they had been formed by spiders dancing. They felt dangerous. Snowball thought they might do him ill just by holding them. But Greysen had told him that this was what he needed to do the dead man's bidding.

'Don't believe me, take it to Old Pickering,' he had said. Pickering was a confessor, known well in York and thereabouts.

But Snowball had had almost a belly-ful of churchmen, so he decided to leave Pickering in peace. He had one more job to do in York, which was to find a friar who would agree to say prayers for –––––'s soul. And by the north gate of the city, just past the Minster, which was covered in wooden scaffolds and builders yelling to one another and laughing in some Danish-sounding dialect Snowball recognized but did not fully understand, he found a friar begging for alms. And they struck a bargain, where the friar would say the prayers and when next he wandered through Ampleforth Snowball would mend his clothes.

'Amen,' said the friar. He seemed happy with his life. Snowball wondered why. He asked the friar to say a prayer for him too, though thinking back to his night with the raven he was not sure whether it could do any good or not.

Then he set out back for Ampleforth, along the muddy track.

Borin was cheerful now, even though the mud of the road splashed up and clung to the legs of them both and it was cold. And Snowball's hips and shoulders ached, very deep inside them, as though someone were in there, tugging on the sinews.

5

SNOWBALL GOT back to Ampleforth two days after he had set out. Jack the Reeve was sitting outside his hut on Borin's waterpail, picking his nose. Snowball thought he must have come on account of the cloak and was ready to tell him to wrap himself in the devil's own horse-blanket if it were all the same, but then he saw Jack looking at him sideways.

He knows, thought Snowball, and he was right.

'Didst tha really meet t' green dog?' asked Jack the Reeve. Snowball wondered if it could have been the fat man or the man with warts or the man who might have been Edwin who told him. But Jack the Reeve refused to say, and nothing Snowball could do then or after would induce him otherwise.

At first Jack the Reeve was excited and demanded Snowball let him come and see the dog and the raven if it came. Snowball told him no, but Jack the Reeve called God forbid, and Snowball sighed and said he might come but he must hide in the hedge-row and bring his father's hat that the old man had worn when he touched the shrine of Thomas at Canterbury.

And he told him that he must meet the dog that night. But as the day went on Jack the Reeve became quieter than normal and as the sun was touching the trees behind the church Jack the Reeve said he remembered he'd told his sister he might call on her that evening.

'Dost tha still want me to go with thee?' said Jack the Reeve.

Snowball looked at him. He knew he did not want to see the dog again. Whether Jack the Reeve was there or not he did not much care.

'You must see to that,' he said. 'I will give no advice to you.'

And suddenly Jack the Reeve looked happy again, and he blessed Snowball and clapped him hard on the back and told him not to mind the cloak the worms had eaten, he would have it when he may. 'And may God prosper thee!' beamed Jack the Reeve, and Snowball nodded quietly.

'In all things,' added Jack the Reeve. And then he said it again, only this time in a lower voice: 'In all things.'

*

The night was clear, the first such one in weeks. Snowball led Borin softly away from his hut towards the road to Gilling, he on foot and his heavy bag slung over Borin's back, and though the moon was thin he thought he could see more stars than he had seen since he was young. He remembered his father telling him about the star-shapes. He could still trace them with his finger. The bear and the crab. The goat and the bull.

And the hunter, with fire in his belt.

Snowball shivered as he remembered what the dog had said.

One burns in the hedgerow, and the other

wanders the fields as a hunter.

He went first to the place where —————'s body had been buried. It was barely a grave at all: just a pile of mismatched stones marking a spot at the first crossroads out of Ampleforth, where older folk said the king's grandfather had hung a traitor in chains. The stone-pile cast a thin shadow in the starlight. Snowball thought back to the day they had put ————— down there. He tried to remember which way had been the head, and which the feet.

He took two paces from the stones in the way he thought the head lay, and scrabbled with his hands. The ground, which had been soft two days past, was starting to freeze. But Snowball scratched away like a dog until he had a hole deep enough to bury Greysen's paper with the strange symbols and tangled words. He placed it in the hole and pushed the cold earth back over it, and stood up and went back to Borin. The horse's breath was steaming, silvered in the starlit air. Snowball took his bag from the horse's back and slung it over his own. Then he climbed into the saddle and set off to meet the green dog and finish what they had begun.

*

Borin, who had been calm until now, stamped and snorted as they neared the place they had seen the dog, and Snowball had to talk to him constantly. 'Calm now, old friend,' he whispered, but his own heart was beating so hard it made the words vibrate as they came out.

At the spot where the raven had screamed and the dog had met him, Snowball stopped and dismounted. He set down his bag and pulled out the things Greysen had told him he must. He told Borin to graze the bank at the roadside, though the horse seemed wary, and backed away down the road, shaking its tail, its eyes wide and darting constantly. Snowball let it go. Then he laid out his things. Four more scraps of parchment, on each of which he had marked in his childlike hand the letters Greysen had told him, the letters of the apostles together, like:

m. m. L. J.

Then with his tailor's chalk Snowball drew a large circle on the ground, and inside it a cross which divided the circle into four. In each of the quarters he placed one of the scraps of parchment, and he weighed them down with pebbles over which he had said his paternoster twelve times.

Then he sat down in the circle. He pulled his hood up and drew his knees towards his chest. And he looked around him at the deserted road and the freezing hedgerow and the stars above him, each of them seeming to flutter as they stared down at him from the heavens.

'Daft,' he said out loud. But he didn't believe it any more than he had before.

6

SNOWBALL WAITED for a long time, watching the stars drift over his head, and he was about to give up when once more the ground seemed to glow. A new noise now filled his head. It was the same feeling as before, but a different sound. It resembled a child grizzling, and Snowball looked around, alarmed at the thought that the dog might visit him in some new form more ghastly than before. But he saw nothing, until after a few minutes there was a rustling from inside the hedgerow and out from the thick-knit branches pushed the head of a small nanny goat, with a tufty white beard and short horn-stubs poking from between her ears.

The nanny goat seemed to be looking for grass on the cold bank, just as Borin had been before the old horse had walked off, and she paid Snowball no mind. Snowball tried to hold his breath and not move. But though the goat's face was lowered he soon found he could hear her bleating, in a voice which fairly rasped through him: 'Nah! Nah!' cried the nanny goat. 'Nah! Nah!'

Then she looked up and Snowball saw with horror that where her eyes should have been were bloody wounds: birds had pecked the eyeballs out. Snowball could see red raw sockets and the ragged pink of torn nerves. He fancied he could see right into her brain. But even so, the nanny seemed to see Snowball through the hideous, ravaged hollows, and she now plodded menacingly towards his circle.

When she came to the edge of it, she stopped short, and instead started to walk around the outside, raising her head at each quarter-turn and crying again: 'Nah! Nah!'

She would not enter the circle, but she cried ever louder, so that Snowball's ears felt they might split inside his head.

'Nah! Nah!'

Snowball shrank back. He knew that the letters in his circle had some power that would keep the nanny goat from harming him, but she was still a frightful sight and he wished she would go away. And he remembered what he had said to the raven and he now repeated it to the goat.

'God forbid thou hast the power to hurt me!' he shouted. 'Begone, foul beast!'

And, just as before, the words seemed to effect a terrible transformation, for now the goat dropped as though she had been shot through the heart with an arrow, and lay still on the ground.

But she did not lie still for long.

7

SLOWLY, WITH a rattle like death, the goat started to transform, and from her skin now rose up a figure in the shape of a man – a man Snowball recognized with horror. He wore fine clothes – finer than anything Snowball had ever stitched or even touched – yet the clothes were shredded and they hung from a body so thin that it seemed to be no more than a skeleton over which was stretched rancid yellowing skin the colour of sour butter.

On his head he wore a fine silk cap, into which were stitched garnets and rubies. But his face had collapsed, its features sagging halfway down the skull, as though they had melted and were dripping as a wax candle does. The man was a king, but he was not any king, thought Snowball. He was one of the Three Dead Kings whose features were painted near the rood in church to put fear into the children and the sinners.

No more than the goat would this dead king enter Snowball's circle. But he turned his hideous face on the tailor and spoke to him, through a jaw that flapped from one hinge on the side of his skull.

'Tailor,' said the dead king. 'Hast thy labour been of use to me?'

Snowball's breath caught in his throat. He had never been so aware of the thickness of his own flesh – of the extraordinary fact of his living body, tight and firm on his bones, held there by his soul, without which all would immediately rot and corrupt. He managed to squeeze out the words:

'Aye,' he said. 'Aye, it has. The priest Greysen and his friends the fat man and the man with warts and the thin man I think is Edwin of Gilling say you – I mean, say –––– – is absolved. And it cost me five shillings, sir, which I had saved for some time. If it pleases you.'

'Oh, it pleases me,' said the dead king. 'And I know tha speakst true, tailor, for I was at thy back when tha scratched in the dirt to bury my absolution, and I felt then thy fear.

'And I feel thy fear yet,' the dead king continued, 'for all around us are the restless dead. Tha canst not see even half of them. There are two more kings with me here now. And as I speak to thee there are three devils here with us, who have been tormenting me ever since thee and I met last. Tha mayst feel their fury in the air, for they know that they have me but little now. For next Monday I shall pass into everlasting joy and leave them.

'I, who was –––––, who did –––– and did not –––––––.'

'You are most welcome, sir,' said Snowball as properly as he could, and he tugged at his hood. But he did not step outside his circle, for he remained wary of the dead king he could see, as well as the others he could not.

And for a time the dead king stared at Snowball, his sunken eyes seeming to thirst for something inside the tailor, yet being unable to take it as they wished.

'There is more to say,' said the dead king, at last. 'I told thee of two other ghosts in this road. They were dangerous to thee but now they are quite harmless. Dost tha care to know who they are?'

Snowball felt he would be told in any wise, so he just nodded and the dead king carried on.

'The first', he said, 'is a soldier. Not from these parts. He strangled a woman who was heavy with child. He will find no remedy till the Day of Judgement, and he is doomed to wander this earth as a bull with no eyes, nor any mouth, nor lugs to hear either.'

Snowball shivered. 'And the second?' he said.

'The second,' said the dead king, 'will find remedy. He is a hunter now, but he was a man of religion once. He is trapped here, but not

DAN JONES

forever. One day a boy will blow a horn and he will be freed.'

'Who is the boy?' asked Snowball.

'Not yet born,' said the dead king. 'Or not yet a man. It is hard for me to say.'

Snowball felt hot everywhere – the burning coming over him as it had before. 'And me?' he said. 'What will happen to me?'

At this the dead king threw back his head and laughed, a sound like the thunder of a thousand birds' wings all beating at once. 'Thee?' he said. 'Th' art a sinner, like all the rest. Tha hast in thy workshop a cloak and cap which tha must return to a man near Alnwick.'

Snowball knew it was so.

'But thy true sin,' said the dead king, 'is on account of me.'

Snowball opened his mouth to ask another

question, but the king spoke again.

'If tha stayst in this place tha wilt be rich. But if tha movest tha wilt be poor.'

And then the dead king said, 'I cannot stay here.' And before Snowball could ask him any more questions, the most pressing of which were what he meant and what could be done with this information, he had vanished. The green light was gone, and the road was silent again, save for the pounding of Snowball's overtaxed heart and the slow mastications made by Borin, who was chewing sticks from the hedge and trying to extract the sap.

Snowball felt his face. It was wet. He wondered if he was melting too, like the dead king – if his eyes had popped and were dribbling down his face. But he had only been crying.

Above him now, the stars were setting.

A weak dawn's grey fingers were starting to claw at the edges of the sky. Snowball set off back towards Ampleforth, stopping on the way to bathe in a stream he knew, where wise folk said the sand and the stones cleansed sin as well as filth from the crevices. And once he was clean he walked on.

As he walked, Borin plodded faithfully on his left side. And on his right – although Snowball could not see it – trotted a baby calf, its face far too big for its body and its eyes and nose and mouth all sealed up and grown over, so that though it shook its bloated head and tried to low and cry and nudge Snowball for his help, it could not. It simply suffered in its dumb, blind, silent way. And when Snowball reached the crossroads where the pile of stones and the scratched-up earth lay, and the memory of the traitor dead in chains hung fetid in the air, the calf vanished, as though it had never been there at all.

By now the low sun was coming up. Snowball was nearly home. He was glad of it, although he knew he would not sleep now for he had work to do that day, all the way back down the road in Gilling.

He would have to get going. Snowball sighed. The ache in his shoulders and his joints had returned and he felt a clammy sensation on his back.

He would not feel well again until long into the next spring.

‡ THE END ‡

A NOTE ON BYLAND ABBEY

When Snowball's story was first written down, Byland Abbey was a famous landmark in northern England. The monastery stood on the edge of the North York Moors, and it consisted of a cluster of well-appointed stone buildings arranged around a magnificent Gothic abbey church, all built on land reclaimed from marshes. Its oldest parts were nearly two and a half centuries old, and the site was massive. Known as one of the three great Yorkshire abbeys (alongside Fountains and Rievaulx), Byland was large enough to house, clothe and feed three hundred men.

By 1400, however, the monastic community there was dwindling. The fourteenth century had been hard on the place: economic decline, decades of war between England and Scotland and the ravages of the Black Death had all reduced numbers. The author of the Byland Abbey ghost stories was one of only about a dozen monks who lived there, served by a handful of assistants known as lay brothers. Despite the grandeur of their surroundings, they were rattling around.

This was all a far cry from the abbey's heyday. Byland's origins lay in the early twelfth century – a time often described as a golden age for monasticism. There had been monks in Europe throughout the Middle Ages, but from the turn of the millennium there was an explosion in abbey-building, and a vigorous trend towards new orders of monasticism. All of the new orders followed a version of the ancient Rule of St Benedict, but their members competed to lead the most austere and godly lives, usually with an emphasis on prayer, work and silence. Although many reformers frowned on luxury and self-indulgence, they tended to live in very impressive surroundings.

Byland's medieval community was founded in 1128 when a group of Savigniac monks banded together at Furness, in Cumberland. (The Savigniacs took their name from their order's home town of Savigny, in Normandy.) In their early years these monks moved extensively around northern England in search of a permanent home. But by the 1150s they had settled in Byland and begun building their monastery there. They had also changed their brand identity, for the Savigniacs had merged with the far bigger and better-known Cistercian order. This was a smart move, for the Cistercians were arguably the most successful order of the High Middle Ages, and their most famous members – such as St Bernard of Clairvaux – were as powerful as popes and kings. Association with the Cistercian movement meant Byland was connected to a sprawling international network of monks and monasteries, stretching from the British Isles to Eastern Europe and the Balkans.

79

Building an abbey like Byland was an expensive business. But successful monasteries tended to be very good at raising money. Some of their wealth came from individual benefactors, who donated money in exchange for the monks saying prayers for their souls, since prayer (as Snowball's story reminds us) was believed to speed a person's passage through purgatory after death. Some of it came from business interests. Byland's most generous benefactors throughout their history were the local Mowbray family, some of whose members were buried in the abbey church. Their most lucrative economic activity was sheep farming. England was known all over Europe for the quality of its wool, which was exported to Flanders and Italy in vast quantities during the fourteenth and fifteenth centuries, where it was manufactured into fine cloth. Much of the wool trade was powered by abbeys such as Byland, on whose lands enormous herds of sheep were grazed. However, the abbey did not depend on wool alone. The monks also managed a sprawling estate in and around north Yorkshire, collecting rents on farms, townhouses and fisheries and even running an iron mine.

So what did Byland look like in 1400? Today the abbey is a ruin. In the Middle Ages, however, it would have been very grand indeed. Its largest feature was the abbey church, completed around 1190, which had a large tower at its eastern end and a glorious rose window on its western front. Adjoining this was one of the biggest cloisters anywhere in England, where brothers could walk, sit in contemplation or make use of little offices for study that were built into one side of the square.

The monastery also had separate quarters for the lay brothers and fully professed monks, which catered to every possible need. There were dormitories and a lavatory block, kitchens, dining rooms and a warming room with a great fireplace to give the brothers some comfort in the cold Yorkshire winters. There was a library, a vestry and a chapter house where the monks could hold meetings. The abbot had private lodgings of his own. The closest comparison today would be with a well-to-do Oxbridge college.

Sadly, almost all of these fine buildings are now lost. All that remains of Byland's walls are shards of stone, which stick out of the ground like jagged, broken teeth. The western front of the abbey church extends to about half its original height, and there are some fine thirteenth-century glazed tiles still in place on what would have been its south transept floor. The footprint of the rest of the monastery is easy to trace, but its life as a place of human activity must be left to archaeology and the imagination.

The reason for Byland's devastation was the English Reformation. In the sixteenth century King Henry VIII withdrew the English Church from obedience to Rome and dissolved the English monasteries. In 1538 Byland's last abbot was forced to disband the community and surrender the monastery. All the valuables were removed and sold. The buildings were ransacked for their lead and glass, and then granted to a local gentleman called Sir William Pickering. Thereafter, Byland remained in private hands until the 1920s, during which time most of its stone was stripped and used to build local houses. Today the site is managed by English Heritage. And, of course, a portion of its library lives on. The British Library holds various chronicles, saints' lives, agricultural treatises and collections of papal letters that were once part of the Byland Abbey collection. Among these is the volume of classical texts on which were written a dozen local ghost stories, including the tale of the tailor, Snowball, and his supernatural encounters, which are set just three miles away from the abbey, around the village of Ampleforth.

THE LATIN TEXT
Edited and annotated by M. R. James

De mirabili certacione inter spiritum et viuentem in tempore regis Ricardi secundi.

Dicitur quod quidam scissor cognomine [blank] Snawball equitando remeauit ad domum suam in ampilforth quadam nocte de Gillyng, et in via audiuit quasi sonitum anates [s]e lauantes [corr. from anas se lauans] in torrente et paulopost aspexit quasi coruum circa faciem suam volantem et descendentem vsque ad terram, alis suis concucientibus solum quasi deberet mori. Qui scissor de equo suo descendit ut caperet coruum et interim vidit sintillas ignis spargentes de lateribus eiusdem corui. Tunc signauit se et prohibuit

Opposite: Text page of ghost story from the Byland Abbey manuscript, c. 1400.

85

eum ex parte dei ne inferret illi dampnum aliquod
illa vice. Qui euolauit cum eiulatu magno quasi
spacium lapidis † enćarđi †.* Tunc iterum ascen-
dit equum suum et paulopost predictus coruus
obuiauit illi in volando et percussit eum in latere
et prostrauit in terra scissorem equitantem de
equo suo. Qui taliter solotenus prostratus iacuit
quasi in extasi et exanimis, valde timens. Tandem
resurgens et constans in fide pugnauit cum eo cum
gladio suo quousque fuerat lassus, et videbatur sibi
quasi percuteret t[er]ricidiu[m] more et prohibuit
eum et defendit ex parte dei, dicens Absit quod
habeas potestatem nocendi mihi in hac vice, sed
recedas. Qui rursus euolauit cum eiulatu horribili
quasi per spacium sagitte volantis. Tercia vero
vice apparuit eidem scissori ferenti crucem gladii
sui super pectus suum pre timore et obuiauit ei
in figura canis anulati.† Quo viso scissor cogitauit

---

* The word is a mystery to me. It seems to begin with E and ends
  with DI. There is a mark of contraction.
† A dog with a chain on its neck.

secum animatus in fide. Quid de me fiet? coni-
urabo eum in nomine trinitatis et per virtutem
sanguinis Ihesu Christi de quinque plagis quod
loqueretur cum eo et ipsum nullatenus lederet sed
staret immobilis et responderet ad interrogata et
diceret ei nomen suum et causam pene sue cum
remedio competenti. Et fecit ita. Qui coniuratus
exalans terribiliter et ingemiscens. Sic et sic feci[*]
et excommunicatus sum pro tali facto. Vadas igitur
ad talem sacerdotem petens absolucionem pro me.
Et oportet me implere nouies viginti missas pro
me celebrandas. et ex duobus vnum eligas. Aut
redeas ad me tali nocte solus, referens respon-
sum de hiis que dixi tibi et docebo te quomodo
sanaberis, et ne timeas visum ignis materialis[†] in

---

[*] Great pains are taken throughout to conceal the name of the
ghost. He must have been a man of quality, whose relatives
might have objected to stories being told about him.

[†] At the end of the story we have 'ne respicias ignem materialem
ista nocte ad minus'. In the Danish tales something like this is
to be found. Kristensen, SAGN OG OVERTRO, 1866, no. 585:
After seeing a phantom funeral the man 'was wise enough to
go to the stove and look at the fire before he saw (candle- or

medio tempore. Aut caro tua putrescet et cutis tua marcescet et dilabetur a te penitus infra breue. Scias igitur quia hodie non audiuisti missam neque ewangelium Iohannis scilicet 'In principio' neque vidisti consecracionem corporis et sanguinis domini obuiaui tibi ad presens, alioquin non haberem plenarie potestatem tibi apparendi. Et cum loqueretur cum eo fuit quasi igneus et conspexit per os eius sua interiora et formauit verba sua in intestinis et non loquebatur lingua. Idem quidem scissor petebat licenciam a predicto spiritu quod poterit habere alium socium secum in redeundo,

lamp-) light. For when people see anything of the kind they are sick if they cannot get at fire before light.' IBID. NO. 371: 'he was very sick when he caught sight of the light.' The same in no. 369. In part II of the same (1888), no. 690: 'When you see anything supernatural, you should peep over the door before going into the house. You must see the light before the light sees you.' Collection of 1883, no. 193: 'When he came home, he called to his wife to put out the light before he came in, but she did not, and he was so sick they thought he would have died.' These examples are enough to show that there was risk attached to seeing light after a ghostly encounter. Does IGNIS MATERIALIS mean simply a fire of wood here?

qui respondit. Non. sed habeas super te quatu-
or euangelia euangelist' et titulum trihumphalem
videlicet Ihesus Nazarenus propter duos alios
spiritus hic commorantes, quorum vnus nequit
loqui coniuratus et est in specie ignis vel dumi et
alter est in figura venatoris, et sunt in obuia valde
periculosi. Facias vlterius fidem huic lapidi quia
non diffamabis ossa mea nisi sacerdotibus cele-
brantibus pro me, et aliis ad quos mitteris ex parte
mea qui possunt mihi prodesse. Qui fidem fecit
lapidi de hoc secreto non reuelando prout supe-
rius est expressum. Demum coniurauit eumdem
spiritum quod iret vsque ad hoggebek* vsque
ad reditum eius. Qui respondit Non. non. non.
eiulando. Cui scissor dixit. Tune vadas ad biland-
banke et letus efficitur. Dictus vero vir infirmaba-
tur per aliquot dies, et statim conualuit et iuit
Eborum ad predictum presbiterum, qui dudum
excommunicauit eum, petens absolucionem. Qui

---

* *I suppose, in order that the ghost might not haunt the road in
the interval before the tailor's return.*

renuit absoluere eum, vocans sibi alium capellanum
ipsum consulendo. At ille vocauit adhuc alium,
et alius tercium de absolucione huius musitantes.*
Qui primo dixit scissor. Domine scitis intersig-
na que suggessi in auribus vestris. Qui respondit. Vere, fili. Tandem post varios tractatus inter
partes isdem scissor satisfecit et soluit quinque
solidos et recepit absolucionem inscriptam in
quadam cedula, adiuratus quod non diffamaret
mortuum sed infoderet illam in sepulcro suo penes
caput eius secrete. Qua accepta ibat ad quendam
fratrem Ric. de Pikeri[n]g nobilem confessorem
sciscitans si dicta absolucio esset sufficiens et legit-
ima. Qui respondit quod sic. Tunc idem scissor
transiuit ad omnes ordines fratrum Eborum et fecit
fere omnes predictas missas celebrari per duos aut
tres dies. et rediens domum fodit predictam absolucionem prout sibi fuerat imperatum in sepulcro.
hiis vero omnibus rite completis venit domum, et

---

* *The reluctance of the priest at York to absolve, and the number*
of advisers called in, testify to the importance of the case.

quidam presumptuosus vicinus eius audiens quod
oportet ipsum referre eidem spiritui que gesserat in
Eborum in tali nocte, adiurauit eum dicens. Absit
quod eas ad predictum spiritum nisi premunias
me de regressu tuo et de die et hora. Qui taliter
constrictus ne displiceret deo premuniit ipsum
excitans a sompno et dixit Iam vado. Si volu-
eris mecum venire, eamus, et dabo tibi partem de
scriptis meis que porto super me propter timores
nocturnos. Cui alter respondit. Vis tu quod eam
tecum? qui respondit. Tu videris. ego nolo prec-
ipere tibi. Tunc alter finaliter dixit.

Vadas ergo in nomine domini et deus expedi-
at te in omnibus.* Quibus dictis venit ad locum
constitutum et fecit magnum circulum crucis,† et
habuit super se quatuor ewangelia et alia sacra
verba, et stetit in medio circuli ponens quatuor

* *The conduct of the officious neighbour who insists upon being
  informed of the tailor's assignation with the ghost and then
  backs out of accompanying him, is amusing.*
† *Whether a circle enclosing a cross or a circle drawn with a
  cross I do not know.*

monilia* in modum crucis in fimbriis eiusdem circuli, in quibus monilibus inscripta erant verba salu-
tifera scilicet Ihesus Nazarenus etc. et expectauit
aduentum spiritus eiusdem. Qui demum venit in
figura capre et ter circa iuit circulum prefatum
dicendo a. a. a. qua coniurata cecidit prona in
terra et resurrexit in figura hominis magne stat-
ure et horribilis et macilenti ad instar vnius regis
mortui depicti.† Et sciscitatus si labor eius ali-
qualiter proficeret ei respondit Laudetur deus quod
sic. et steti ad dorsum hora nona quando infodis-
ti absolucionem meam in sepulcro et timuisti. nec
mirum, quia tres diaboli fuerunt ibidem presentes,
qui omnimodis tormentis puniebant me postquam
coniurasti me prima vice vsque ad absolucionem
meam, suspicantes se permodicum tempus me in
sua custodia habituros ad puniendum. Scias igitur
quod die lune proxime futura ego cum aliis triginta

---

* Small 'reliquaries' such as could be worn on the person.
† I think the allusion is to the pictures of the Three Living and
  Three Dead so often found painted on church-walls. The Dead
  and Living are often represented as kings.

spiritibus ibimus in gaudium sempiternum. Tu
ergo vadas ad torrentem talem et inuenies lapidem
latum quem eleues et sub illo lapide capias petram
arenaciam. laues eciam totum corpus cum aqua
et frica cum petra et sanaberis infra paucos dies.[*]
Qui interrogatus de nominibus duorum spirituum
respondit. Non possum dicere tibi illorum nomina.
Iterum inquisitus de statu eorundem asseruit quod
unus illorum erat secularis et bellicosus et non fuit
de ista patria, et occidit mulierem pregnantem et
non habebit remedium ante diem iudicii, et videbis
eum in figura bouiculi sine ore et oculis et auribus,
et nullatenus quamuis coniuretur poterit loqui. Et
alius erat religiosus in figura venatoris cum cornu
comantis, et habebit remedium et coniurabitur per
quendam puerulum nondum pubescentem domino
disponente. Postea inquisiuit eundem spiritum de
suo proprio statu. qui respondit ei. Tu detines
iniuste capucium et togam quondam amici et socii

[*] *The need of a prescription for healing the tailor was due to the
blow in the side which the crow (raven?) had given him.*

93

tui in guerra vltra mare. Satisfacies ergo ei vel
grauiter lues. Qui respondit Nescio vbi est. Cui
alter respondit In tali villa habitat prope castel-
lum de Alnewyke. Vlterius inquisitus Quod est
culpa mea maxima? respondit. Maxima culpa tua
est causa mei. Cui viuus Quo modo et qualiter
hoc? Dixit Quia populus peccat de te menciens
et alios mortuos scandalizans et dicens Aut est ille
mortuus qui coniurabatur aut ille vel ille. Et inquisiuit eundem spiritum Quid igitur fiet? Reuelabo
ergo nomen tuum. Qui respondit Non. Sed si
manseris in tali loco eris diues et in tali loco
eris pauper, et habes aliquos inimicos.* Tandem
spiritus respondit Non possum longius stare et
loqui tibi. Quibus discedentibus ab inuicem predictus surdus et mutus et cecus bouiculus ibat
cum viuente vsque ad villam de ampilford, quem

---

* This does not seem to follow logically upon the prohibition to
  tell the ghost's name. I take it as advice to the tailor to change
  his abode. 'If you take up your abode – reside – in such a place
  you will prosper; if in such a place you will be poor; and you
  have some enemies (where you now are).'

coniurauit omnibus modis quibus sciuit, sed nullo modo potuit respondere. Spiritus autem alius per ipsum adiutus consuluit eum quod poneret optima sua scripta in suo capite dum dormiret et non dicas amplius vel minus quam que precipio tibi, et respicias ad terram et ne respicias ignem materialem ista nocte ad minus. Qui rediens domum per dies aliquot grauiter egrotabat.

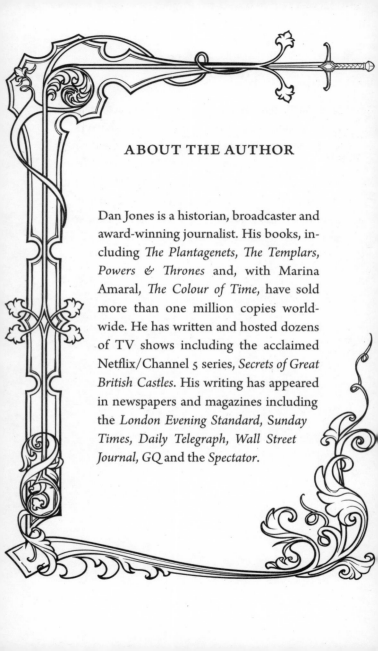

ABOUT THE AUTHOR

Dan Jones is a historian, broadcaster and award-winning journalist. His books, including *The Plantagenets*, *The Templars*, *Powers & Thrones* and, with Marina Amaral, *The Colour of Time*, have sold more than one million copies worldwide. He has written and hosted dozens of TV shows including the acclaimed Netflix/Channel 5 series, *Secrets of Great British Castles*. His writing has appeared in newspapers and magazines including the *London Evening Standard*, *Sunday Times*, *Daily Telegraph*, *Wall Street Journal*, *GQ* and the *Spectator*.